For Professor Martin Salisbury and the
amazing tutors at Cambridge School of Art

First published in Great Britain in 2019 by

Andersen Press Ltd., 20 Vauxhall Bridge Road,

London SW1V 2SA.

Copyright © Margarita Surnaite, 2019.

The right of Margarita Surnaite to be identified

as the author and illustrator of this work

has been asserted by her in accordance with

the Copyright, Designs and Patents Act, 1988.

Printed and bound in China.

First edition

British Library Cataloguing in Publication Data available.

ISBN 978 1 78344 684 1

THE LOST BOOK

Margarita Surnaite

ANDERSEN PRESS

Henry lived in Rabbit Town with
his mum and dad, big sister Kate,
and little sister Amy.

In Rabbit Town, books were EVERYWHERE.
Rabbit adventures, rabbit history, rabbit food.

And all rabbits loved books...
except for Henry.

"What's so special about all these books?" he wondered.

"Games and real adventures are much more fun."

But then Henry found
the Lost Book.

It was not
a rabbit book.

"How did it get here?"
thought Henry.

"Did someone lose it?
Are they looking for it?"
But most of all, Henry
was curious to know...

... where it
had come
from.

He set off to find the owner
of the Lost Book.

But the creatures he met did not seem to care.

And they did not notice Henry,
who was beginning to feel
a little bit lost himself.

Just as he was about to lose hope,

Henry started to read the Lost Book and something amazing happened...

... almost.

"Excuse me," said the little creature. "I think you lost this."

It turned out there was one nice thing about getting lost:

being found.

Henry spent the afternoon
with his new friend.

She showed him
around the city.

And he found out about all of
her favourite things.

He enjoyed himself so much, he forgot all about the Lost Book.

"Oh, my mum is here. I have to go," said the little creature.

Henry had a gift for his new friend, so she wouldn't forget him.

She had been so good at finding Henry and taking care of him, he knew the Lost Book would be in good hands.

"Mum, Dad, look –
it's a book!"

"You won't believe who I met today. He's sitting right..."

"Where did he go?"

"Henry! Where have you been?" asked his dad.

Henry just hugged everybody tightly.

That night, for the first time,
it was Henry who told the bedtime story.

An adventure so exciting,
it could have been in a book.